THE GREAT STONE FACE

Design: Paul Higdon, Andrea Boven

1 2 3 4 5 6 7 8 9 10 Printing/Year 01 00 99 98 97

Text © 1997 by Penelope J. Stokes
Illustrations © 1997 by Greg Dearth

ISBN: 1-56476-544-X
Suggested Subject Heading: GIFT; INSPIRATIONAL

Published by Chariot Books
All rights reserved. Printed in Canada.

Chariot Books is an imprint of ChariotVictor Publishing,
a division of Cook Communications, Colorado Springs, Colorado 80918
Cook Communications, Paris, Ontario
Kingsway Communications, Eastbourne, England

NATHANIEL HAWTHORNE

THE GREAT STONE FACE

Abridged by PENELOPE J. STOKES
Illustrated by GREG DEARTH

ChariotVICTOR
PUBLISHING
A DIVISION OF COOK COMMUNICATIONS

*L*ate one afternoon, just as the sun was going down, a child sat with his mother in the doorway of their cottage, looking up at the mountains. Birds flitted across the valley, singing their evensong. Above them, rugged cliffs rose to meet the darkening sky, silent and strong and familiar. The descending sun sent a shaft of crimson light over the valley and played across the cliffs to the east.

Ernest—for that was the boy's name—squeezed his mother's hand and pointed to the mountains. "Look, Mother! Look!" he whispered. "The Great Stone Face is coming to life!"

His mother smiled down at her child and then looked up to the crest of the mountain. Indeed, the rock formation high in the eastern ridge did appear alive, struck as it was by the rays of the sun. A huge granite forehead protruded from the mountain, a hundred feet in height. One long boulder formed the nose, and two enormous stones created lips that, if they could have spoken, would have rattled the valley with their thunder. But the eyes! The eyes were most alive, especially at this time of the day, when the sun threw magical lights and shadows into their crevices.

It was true that if you drew too near to the stony face in the mountain, you would lose sight of the eyes and nose and lips and brow. You would see only a rubble of stones, one piled upon another. But as you retreated again to the lowlands, the face would once more appear, surrounded by light and mist, casting its watchful gaze over the valley.

To the people who lived in its shadow, the Great Stone Face was not just a natural monument, carved into the

mountain by the hand of the Creator. It was a living benediction, an eternal blessing upon their lives. When they looked upon it, they felt as if God himself were smiling down upon them in the image of the Great Stone Face.

And God had, indeed, blessed them. The valley was fertile and productive, supporting a rich harvest of crops and large herds of cattle and sheep. Thousands of people lived in the flatland between the eastern and the western mountains and thousands more in the foothills, where clear rivers plunged into waterfalls and powered the machines that ran their factories and provided energy for their mills.

Life in the Valley of the Great Stone Face was a happy life, especially for the children who grew up seeing it every day. Its features were warm and comforting and noble, teaching without words the value of love and acceptance and harmony among all people. Like a devoted and protective parent, it stood over them all and watched them grow, rejoicing when the boys and girls under its care grew into men and women of virtue and faith.

Everyone loved the Great Stone Face. But no one in the valley loved it more than Ernest.

"Tell me the story again, Mother," he pleaded as they sat

watching the sun descend across the valley. "Tell me the story of the Great Stone Face."

Ernest's mother laughed. "You know the story by heart, my child. You know it as well as I do."

"But I want to hear it again."

The mother drew her child into her arms and kissed the top of his head. "All right," she said as she settled him into her lap. "Once more, and then to bed."

Ernest smiled up at her and laid his head on her shoulder as she began.

"Many years ago, before my mother or her mother or her grandmother was born, a tribe of Indians inhabited this valley, tilling their fields and tending their flocks much as we do. But the story goes back even further. They heard the tale from their parents and grandparents, who, it is said, heard it from the murmuring wind and the rustling trees.

"They too lived under the blessing of the Great Stone Face, for he has been up there on the mountain longer than anyone has ever lived down here in the valley. And according to their legends, one day—no one knows when—a child would be born in this valley, a very special child, destined to be the greatest, noblest person who ever walked among us.

The prophecy says that when he comes and is grown to manhood, his words will be full of truth and wisdom, and his heart will be full of love."

Ernest turned in his mother's arms and looked up into her face. "And the best part of the story—" he prompted.

"The best part of the story," she continued, stroking his hair, "is that this man—this noble, gracious, wise man—will be known to all, for he will bear in his own likeness the exact image of the Great Stone Face in the mountain."

Ernest straightened up in her lap, his eyes bright with anticipation. "Oh, Mother," he whispered, "I hope I will live to see him. If I ever met a man with a face like that, I would love him—I know I would."

Then his expression darkened and he looked intently at her. "But everyone does not believe the prophecy," he murmured. "I have heard people in the valley talking about it, and some of them don't believe it will ever be fulfilled."

Ernest's mother sighed. "It is a very old legend, son. People have been waiting for generations to see the man who would be the living image of the Great Stone Face. They have watched and waited until they are tired of waiting, and they have met no one who is greater or nobler

than any of their neighbors."

Ernest looked up at her, puzzled. He could not imagine that anyone would grow tired of believing in the Great Stone Face. "It will happen," the boy said firmly. "It will. And I believe I will be alive to see it."

Ernest's mother gazed out across the valley to the eastern slopes, where the Great Stone Face was now shadowed in darkness. "Perhaps you shall," she said quietly. "Perhaps you shall."

And so Ernest believed, and continued to believe. And he never forgot the story that his mother told him.

One spring, when Ernest was no longer a boy, but yet not quite a man, a rumor went through the valley that the person from the legends, the one whose face bore the likeness of the Great Stone Face, had appeared at last.

Many years before, a young man had left the valley to seek his fortune in a distant seaport. The man now owned a fleet of whaling vessels and sold the whale oil at a great profit. He had accumulated much wealth, and his reputation as a generous benefactor to the poor had spread far and wide. At last he was returning to the valley of his youth, to live out his days in the shadow of the Great Stone Face. Surely his very presence in the valley would make life better for all of them. His name, they said, was Mr. Gathergold.

All the people of the valley watched in awe as Mr. Gathergold's house began to be built. Stone by stone it rose, on a choice piece of land near the foothills of the mountains. Under the very shadow of the Great Stone Face, the house took shape—not a humble cottage like most of the dwellings in the valley, but a large and imposing castle, created from granite cut out of the mountain itself.

The house was a wonder to behold, with tall polished pillars that gleamed like marble, leaded glass windows that reflected the sun, and heavy walnut doors studded with silver. Only the workmen were permitted inside, but word quickly spread around the valley that the interior of the house was even more glorious than the exterior. Even the bedroom had gilded moldings, the people said, and marble floors and glittering chandeliers.

When the house was at last completed, it stood like a monument to Mr. Gathergold's success—a palace fit for a nobleman or a prince.

And then the great man himself came to occupy his mansion.

On the day of Mr. Gathergold's arrival, the entire population of the village turned out to welcome him home. He arrived in a polished carriage with golden wheels and four white horses—a finer rig than anyone in the valley had ever seen.

As the rich man drove through the streets and received the applause and adulation of the crowd, Ernest hung back a bit and watched.

The man had a low forehead, small, sharp eyes, and thin lips which disappeared completely when he pressed them together. Thin as a scarecrow, Mr. Gathergold was, with puckered skin that hung on him like an oversized suit and hands as skinny as bird claws.

Yet, to Ernest's surprise, when the rich man leaned his head out the carriage window and waved a claw toward the crowd, the people began to cheer, "Here is the great Mr. Gathergold. Look! He is the very image of the Great Stone Face!"

By the roadside, there happened to be a homeless beggar woman and her two children—not natives of the valley, but strangers from some far-off region. As the carriage rolled toward them, they held out their hands, begging for some small bit of charity to help them keep body and soul together. Mr. Gathergold never looked at them, but his clawlike hand reached out the window and tossed a few coins in their direction—not gold coins, or even silver, but only a few copper pennies, barely enough for a single loaf of bread.

And still, as the carriage rolled out of town and up toward the palace in the foothills, people ran behind it, crying, "The Great Stone Face! The Great Stone Face!"

With a heart full of sadness, Ernest turned his eyes from the scene and looked up to the eastern ridge. There, in the gathering mist, the familiar face he knew and loved so well still smiled down at him. The broad granite lips never moved, but in his soul Ernest heard the words: "He will come; fear not, Ernest! The man will come."

And so young Ernest went home to his mother disappointed. But he took with him the beggar woman and her two children, to share a simple meal of stew and fresh-baked bread.

The years went by, and Ernest still lived with his mother in the log cottage where he had been born. As he grew toward manhood and his mother became older, he remained with her and took a job in the fields to support them both. All their neighbors and friends praised Ernest for being a loving and dutiful son, and for not leaving the valley to seek his fortune like so many other young people had done.

But Ernest's love for his mother was only one reason he chose to stay. The other was the influence of the Great Stone Face.

Ernest was not an educated youth, but over the years the Great Stone Face became a kind of tutor for him, silently encouraging him to learn and grow, to read and exercise his mind. The little cottage that Ernest shared with his mother was filled with books of all kinds, and every evening as the sun set across the craggy countenance on the mountain, Ernest would sit at his doorstep in the waning light and read poetry and history, fiction and philosophy.

Ernest's most valuable lessons, however, were not found in his books. From the Great Stone Face itself he learned to be loving, kind, compassionate, and generous to those around him. He spent hours gazing upon the great face, imagining in his mind what it would say to him if it could speak. After a while he began to think that it did speak to him—not in words, but in his heart, as it had one time before. He beheld the noble features beaming down at him, and he knew without a doubt that the Great Stone Face loved him.

Mr. Gathergold had long since died—in poverty, the people of the valley said. Not content with enough wealth to last a hundred men a hundred lifetimes, he had invested every cent in a luxury ship, the finest vessel ever to sail the oceans. When, on its maiden voyage, it sank to the bottom of the sea, Mr. Gathergold's fortune sank with it. He died alone, a bitter, penniless miser with only the roof over his head, and even his magnificent palace had now gone to ruin.

When people spoke of Mr. Gathergold, they shook their heads, sighed, and said they couldn't understand how anyone could ever have mistaken the old penny-pincher for the Great Stone Face. No one but a fool could look upon that shriveled, mean-eyed skinflint and think that he could have been the fulfillment of the prophecy.

No, Mr. Gathergold was not the Great Stone Face. The prophecy had yet to be fulfilled.

Then, a little more than a year after Ernest's mother had died, a report began to circulate among the people that the true image of the Great Stone Face had been found. A native-born son of the valley had left years before to enlist as a soldier, and after many hard-fought battles, he had become a hero. His name was General Warlord, and he was coming home to the valley to live out his days in peace.

The General's aide arrived, and the village leaders gathered with him to plan a festival in honor of the General's coming. Old school friends of the General's testified that, even as a boy, his countenance had borne the nobility and strength of the Great Stone Face. Anticipation rippled through the village. Even those who claimed not to believe the prophecy at all began gazing up at the face in the mountain, so that they would know exactly how General Warlord looked.

On the day of the General's arrival, Ernest, like all the other people of the valley, left his work and went to the glade in the forest, where an enormous banquet had been prepared.

The tables had been arranged in a clearing surrounded by trees, except for one break in the woods through which a distant view of the Great Stone Face was visible. As they listened to speeches and toasts and waited for General Warlord to make his appearance, the crowd grew in number, pushing forward toward the head tables to get a better look at the man who bore the image of the Great Stone Face.

Ernest, who was a quiet and unobtrusive man, found himself far back in the crowd, and when the General arrived, he could see little of the man's face. But the cry drifted back from the front of the throng, "It is the same face! The face in the mountain! The General is the exact image of the Great Stone Face!"

"And why shouldn't he be?" a man at Ernest's elbow said. "He is, after all, the greatest man of this or any other age."

Now Ernest had always imagined that when the prophecy finally came true, the long-awaited person would be a man of character, a man of peace, speaking wisdom, doing good, and making people happy. General Warlord was a man of battle, who had gained his fame through bloodshed. But in his simple faith, Ernest conceded that perhaps the providence of God might work in a way he could not understand, choosing its own method of blessing humankind. Divine wisdom might, after all, use even a bloody sword and a warlike heart to accomplish its purposes.

He pressed forward for a better look. There, on the platform, stood General Warlord, the gold braid on his uniform sparkling in the sun, medals gleaming on his chest. Behind him, through the break in the trees, the great face in the mountain gazed down upon the festival.

Ernest stared at the Great Stone Face, then at the General, then back again at the mountain. Was there, indeed, such a resemblance? The General's face had a war-weary, weather-beaten look, a frowning brow that reflected an iron will. And yet none of the nobler features of the Great Stone Face were

present—none of the love and compassion, none of the sympathy and protectiveness that Ernest had always depended upon.

"This is not the man of the prophecy," Ernest sighed. He closed his eyes and shook his head in disappointment. "How long must we wait until we see the true image of the Great Stone Face?"

Late afternoon mists had gathered around the upper cliffs of the mountainside. Ernest looked up again to see the Great Stone Face smiling down at him—like a magnificent angel, robed in clouds of gold and purple. Once more he felt hope surge in his heart, the hope that all was not lost, that someday the long-awaited one would come. As he watched, the light shifted, and although the lips never moved, once more he heard the promise in his soul: "Fear not, Ernest. He will come."

Many years passed by, and Ernest matured into middle age. He worked hard at his humble labors and maintained his faith that someday he would see the fulfillment of the prophecy about the Great Stone Face.

Quietly, by degrees, Ernest had become known among the people of the valley. He was still the same simple-hearted man. But he had given so much of his life to study—and to his unshakable hope in the Great Stone Face—that people often said he seemed like a man who had talked with the angels and absorbed their wisdom in the process. He lived a calm and faith-filled life, and not a day went by that Ernest did not make the world better by helping those around him.

In addition to his good deeds, Ernest was sought out for his insight. He would not have called himself a teacher, and perhaps the people of the valley did not understand why they found his words so attractive. But whether they understood or not, they came to him for advice and counsel, and they discovered in him a depth of wisdom, simplicity, and truth that no other human lips had ever spoken.

When the enthusiasm for General Warlord had cooled, the people readily acknowledged that they had made a mistake in assuming him to be the human incarnation of the Great Stone Face. But when a new rumor arose that another native of the valley had achieved greatness, they once again began to proclaim that the fulfillment of the prophecy had finally come.

This third man possessed neither the wealth of Mr. Gathergold nor the might of General Warlord, but he had something even more powerful—the gift of persuasion. He was called Senator Stonewall, and he had made a name for himself in law and politics. A senior statesman, Stonewall had the reputation for being able to convince his listeners of anything. His voice was like a magic instrument; sometimes it rumbled like thunder, sometimes it warbled sweetly like the song of birds. And with it he could make wrong seem right and right seem wrong. If he said that day was dark and night was bright, people would believe him, even if their senses told them something entirely different.

With such an ability to persuade his listeners, Senator Stonewall had risen to a position of great influence in the government. Now he was traveling far and wide, urging people everywhere to elect him President of all the land. And in his travels, he was returning to the valley of his boyhood.

When Ernest heard about Stonewall, his heart swelled with hope. Perhaps here, at last, was the fulfillment of the legends about the distinguished man who would bear the image of the Great Stone Face.

With all his neighbors and friends, Ernest went out to the border of the village to welcome the great statesman to the valley. There was a marvelous parade, with the town fathers on horseback and a brass band playing. It was a brilliant sight, a spectacle that stirred the blood and made even Ernest hope that the day had finally come when the prophecy would be fulfilled.

Some of the riders in the Senator's procession carried huge banners showing Stonewall's face next to the image in the mountain. If the pictures could be believed, there was, indeed, a great resemblance between the two. And when the band played its soul-thrilling melodies, the music echoed back from the mountains—as if the Great Stone Face itself were singing the praises of the Senator's triumph.

"Hurrah!" the people shouted as the Senator rode past. "Hurrah for Senator Stonewall! Hurrah for the Great Stone Face!"

And Ernest himself, compelled by the depth of his hope, threw his own hat into the air and shouted, "Hurrah!"

Here he is!" cried a man who stood next to Ernest in the crowd. "There! Look at Stonewall, and then at the face in the mountain. They are as alike as twin brothers!"

Ernest looked. But for all his hope, his heart sank within him. There was a similarity, to be sure: the Senator had the same broad brow and strong features, the same chiseled nose and powerful mouth. But something was missing. Deep in Senator Stonewall's eyes, Ernest saw the look of a man who was weary with life, a man who had no faith of his own. It was the expression of a child who has grown bored with his toys and seeks something else—anything else—to distract him from his boredom.

Ernest looked at the Senator long and hard, for he desperately wanted to believe that this time the prophecy had come true. But try as he might, he could not see in the

statesman's expression what he had always found in the face on the mountain—love, compassion, tenderness, nobility of spirit. Ernest's heart wrenched with discouragement, for the man before him might have been the Great Stone Face come to life—if only he had lived for others rather than for his own ambition.

"Confess it," Ernest's neighbor urged, prodding him in the ribs. "Isn't this man the very image of the Old Man on the Mountain?"

But Ernest shook his head. "No," he said bluntly. "He is not the one." And as the neighbor protested, Ernest turned sadly away. This was the worst disappointment of all—to find a man who could have been the fulfillment of the prophecy, if only his heart had been right.

Ernest stood aside and let the Senator's procession pass. When the horses had gone by, the dust settled, and the music of the brass bands faded into a distant echo, Ernest looked once more up to the eastern ridge of the mountain, where the grandeur of the Great Stone Face still looked down solemnly over the valley.

Suddenly Ernest remembered what his mother had told him so many years ago—how many people became discouraged

and lost faith
in the fulfillment of the
prophecy. And for the first time in
his life, Ernest could understand how they could give up. He
had spent his life waiting, believing, hoping. Three times
now he had let himself believe that the fulfillment of the
prophecy had actually come to pass. And three times he had
been disappointed.

"I am here, Ernest," the massive stone lips seemed to
say. "I have waited longer than you have. For untold centuries
I have waited, and yet I am not weary. Have faith, Ernest.
Have faith, and fear not; the man will come."

As men and women get older, time seems to hurry by faster and faster, and so it seemed to Ernest as his hair turned to silver and wrinkles lined his cheeks and brow. But he had not grown old in vain; there were more pure thoughts in his mind than gray hairs on his head, more wisdom in his heart than wrinkles on his face.

Ernest had not sought or desired fame, but it had come to him nevertheless. His wisdom was known and respected far beyond the reaches of his little valley. College professors, statesmen, and writers traveled to the Valley of the Great Stone Face to meet Ernest and talk with him. But for all the attention Ernest received, it never seemed to change him. He remained unaffected by the adulation of the multitudes, unmoved by their flattery. He received them all with sincerity and simplicity, speaking to them in quiet tones of the faith that sustained his life, of the truths he had learned and lived for so many years. And when they left him, full of wonder at the wisdom of a modest, uneducated man, many of them looked upward to the hills, to the Great Stone Face, and imagined that they had seen that face before—though none of them could remember where.

While Ernest had been growing up and growing old, a poet had risen to prominence in the world beyond the valley. His writing was acclaimed throughout the land for its depth and nobility, and especially for its descriptions of a magnificent rock formation in the mountain regions of his childhood. His poems enabled people to see the beauty of the earth as never before, and to appreciate the wonder of the God who created the world. Many said that as the last, best touch to his Creation, God had given this poet the ability to interpret the work of God's own hands, to make the loveliness of Creation live anew for all who read his verses.

The writings of this poet found their way into Ernest's hands. He would sit, as was his custom, in the doorway of his little log cottage, reading and rereading them, marveling at the nobility and compassion and truth contained in the words.

"Oh, Majestic Friend," Ernest murmured to the Great Stone Face, "is this not a man who is worthy to bear your image?"

And the Face smiled down upon him, but answered not a word.

Now the poet, although he lived far away, had heard of the wisdom of a simple man in the valley of his childhood— a man by the name of Ernest. He traveled to the valley and, rather than seeking a room at the nearby hotel, asked directions to Ernest's cottage.

When he arrived, he saw an old man sitting in the doorway, reading from a book, and looking with love and longing up to the mountain, toward the Great Stone Face.

"Good evening," the poet said. "Would you be able to give a traveler a night's lodging?"

"Certainly," Ernest answered. "Sit down and make yourself comfortable."

The poet sat beside Ernest, and they began to talk. Never had the poet encountered anyone with such purity of thought and depth of faith and wisdom as this humble man. And never had Ernest felt himself so drawn to the ideas and images which the poet discussed. As they talked, Ernest listened intently, and he imagined that the Great Stone Face, too, was leaning forward to listen.

"Who are you, my gifted friend?" he asked at last.

The poet laid a hand upon the book Ernest held. "Have you read these poems?"

Ernest nodded.

"If you have read them, you know me—for I wrote them."

Ernest gazed intently into the poet's face, then lifted his eyes to the Face upon the mountain. He shook his head uncertainly, and his shoulders sagged.

"Why are you sad?" the poet asked.

"Because," Ernest replied, "all my life I have waited for an ancient prophecy to come true. When I read your poems, I imagined that you might, at last, be the one to fulfill it."

The poet smiled faintly. "You hoped to find in me the image of the Great Stone Face," he said quietly. "And you are disappointed, as you were with Mr. Gathergold, General Warlord, and Senator Stonewall. But I am not the man you seek. I am afraid you must add my name as well to the list of disappointments, for I am not worthy to bear the likeness of the Man in the Mountain."

"But why?" Ernest protested, pointing to the book of poems. "These thoughts are noble and divine."

"They have a touch of the divine," the poet answered.

"But I must confess that my words are often greater than the faith in my own heart. I sometimes lack the hope, the love, the nobility that even my own poems reflect."

Tears filled the poet's eyes, and together he and Ernest wept that the prophecy had not been fulfilled, after all.

As the sun was setting, Ernest rose and turned to the poet. "Come with me," he said. "In the evenings, I meet with people from the valley to talk with them and share what is in my heart and mind. It seems to comfort them and strengthen their faith. I have been so deeply touched by your

poems that I would like for them to meet you."

Together they walked to the clearing in the woods where, years before, the people had acclaimed General Warlord as the image of the Great Stone Face. Tonight there was no festival, no banquet, no brass bands or banners—just a bright moon rising over the Face in the mountain, shining down into the little glade.

People were scattered throughout the clearing—some sitting on the grass, others standing in a semicircle around a little rise in the center of the glade. Ernest stood on the hill where he could be seen and heard by all the people, and began to speak.

The poet watched and listened, amazed at the truth which came from Ernest's lips. This simple man, with his simple words, spoke of a faith so deep and pure, so compassionate and humble, that the people could not help being encouraged and strengthened in their own hope. Ernest was not a persuasive speaker or a powerful man, but love flowed out from him and comforted everyone who listened to him.

And as the poet watched, his eyes again filled with tears—not tears of sadness this time, but tears of joy. Never had he heard words of such wisdom, or such worthiness.

Never had he seen a face of such nobility as Ernest's face, filled with mercy and with grace.

The poet's gaze lifted to the great granite formation in the mountain overhead. The moonlight shone upon the massive features, and the mists of evening gathered around its head like a glorious cloud of silver hair.

Then suddenly, he knew the truth. "Behold!" he cried. "Look up, and see! Ernest is himself the likeness of the Great Stone Face!"

All the people turned to look, and they saw that what the poet said was true. The old, old prophecy was fulfilled—not in a man of great wealth, military might, or political power, but in their own Ernest, with his deep love and faith, and his simple wisdom.

Ernest finished speaking, took the arm of his friend, and walked in silence back to his humble cottage. And that night he prayed, as he had prayed all his life, that someday a better, nobler, wiser man would appear, bearing the image of the Great Stone Face.

NATHANIEL HAWTHORNE (1804—1864)

Nathaniel Hawthorne, best known for his novels *The Scarlet Letter* and *The House of the Seven Gables*, was born in Salem, Massachusetts in 1804. His life and work reflect the powerful influence of the religious mood and the cultural heritage of nineteenth-century New England. Educated at Bowdoin College, where he was a classmate of Longfellow's, Hawthorne absorbed the legacy of faith and culture that surrounded him. Both in life and in reading, he came to understand the depth and complexity of the human soul, the duplicity of the human heart, the divine significance of human life, and the hand of God in the midst of all creation.

Perhaps more than any of his stories, "The Great Stone Face" demonstrates Hawthorne's conviction that the spark of the eternal God glows in the humblest expressions of human life. The ancient prophecy—that the Great Stone Face would one day come to life in a person of great honor and nobility—finds its fulfillment not in people who are powerful according to the world's standards, but in one who exhibits Christlike love, integrity, and honesty.